The White People

Frances Hodgson Burnett

Contents

THE WHITE PEOPLE

BY

Frances Hodgson Burnett

TO LIONEL

"The stars come nightly to the sky;
The tidal wave unto the sea;
Nor time, nor space, nor deep, nor high
Can keep my own away from me."

CHAPTER I

Perhaps the things which happened could only have happened to me. I do not know. I never heard of things like them happening to any one else. But I am not sorry they did happen. I am in secret deeply and strangely glad. I have heard other people say things--and they were not always sad people, either--which made me feel that if they knew what I know it would seem to them as though some awesome, heavy load they had always dragged about with them had fallen from their shoulders. To most people everything is so uncertain that if they could only see or hear and know something clear they would drop upon their knees and give thanks. That was what I felt myself before I found out so strangely, and I was only a girl. That is why I intend to write this down as well as I can. It will not be very well done, because I never was clever at all, and always found it difficult to talk.

I say that perhaps these things could only have happened to me, because, as I look back over my life, I realize that it has always been a rather curious one. Even when those who took care of me did not know I was thinking at all, I had begun to wonder if I were not different from other children. That was, of course, largely because Muircarrie Castle was in such a wild and remote part of Scotland that when my few relations felt they must pay me a visit as a mere matter of duty, their journey from London, or their pleasant places in the south of England, seemed to them like a pilgrimage to a sort of savage land; and when a conscientious one brought a child to play with me, the little civilized creature was as frightened of me as I was of it. My shyness and fear of its strangeness made us both dumb. No doubt I seemed like a new breed of inoffensive little barbarian, knowing no tongue but its own.

A certain clannish etiquette made it seem necessary that a relation should pay me a visit sometimes, because I was in a way important. The huge, frowning feudal castle standing upon its battlemented rock was mine; I was a great heiress, and I was, so to speak, the chieftainess of the clan. But I was a plain, undersized little child, and had no attraction for any one but Jean Braidfute, a distant cousin, who took care of me, and Angus Macayre, who took care of the library, and who was a distant relative also. They were both like me in the fact that they were not given to speech; but sometimes we talked to one another, and I knew they were fond of me, as I was fond of them. They were really all I had.

When I was a little girl I did not, of course, understand that I was an important person, and I could not have realized the significance of being an heiress. I had always lived in the castle, and was used to its hugeness, of which I only knew corners. Until I was seven years old, I think, I imagined all but very poor people lived in castles and were saluted by every one they passed. It seemed probable that all little girls had a piper who strode up and down the terrace and played on the bagpipes when guests were served in the dining-hall.

My piper's name was Feargus, and in time I found out that the guests from London could not endure the noise he made when he marched to and fro, proudly swinging his kilts and treading like a stag on a hillside. It was an insult to tell him to stop playing, because it was his religion to believe that The Muircarrie must be piped proudly to; and his ancestors had been pipers to the head of the clan for five generations. It was his duty to march round the dining-hall and play while the guests feasted, but I was obliged in the end to make him believe that he could be heard better from the terrace--because when he was outside his music was not spoiled by the sound of talking. It was very difficult, at first. But because I was his chieftainess, and had learned how to give orders in a rather proud, stern little voice, he knew he must obey.

Even this kind of thing may show that my life was a peculiar one; but the strangest part of it was that, while I was at the head of so many people, I did not really belong to any one, and I did not know that this was unusual. One of my early memories is that I heard an under-nursemaid say to another this curious thing: "Both her father and mother were dead when she was born." I did not even know that was a remarkable thing to say until I was several years older and Jean Braidfute told me what had been meant.

My father and mother had both been very young and beautiful and wonderful.

It was said that my father was the handsomest chieftain in Scotland, and that his wife was as beautiful as he was. They came to Muircarrie as soon as they were married and lived a splendid year there together. Sometimes they were quite alone, and spent their days fishing or riding or wandering on the moor together, or reading by the fire in the library the ancient books Angus Macayre found for them. The library was a marvelous place, and Macayre knew every volume in it. They used to sit and read like children among fairy stories, and then they would persuade Macayre to tell them the ancient tales he knew--of the days when Agricola forced his way in among the Men of the Woods, who would die any savage death rather than be conquered. Macayre was a sort of heirloom himself, and he knew and believed them all.

I don't know how it was that I myself seemed to see my young father and mother so clearly and to know how radiant and wildly in love they were. Surely Jean Braidfute had not words to tell me. But I knew. So I understood, in a way of my own, what happened to my mother one brilliant late October afternoon when my father was brought home dead--followed by the guests who had gone out shooting with him. His foot had caught in a tuft of heather, and his gun in going off had killed him. One moment he had been the handsomest young chieftain in Scotland, and when he was brought home they could not have let my mother see his face.

But she never asked to see it. She was on the terrace which juts over the rock the castle is built on, and which looks out over the purple world of climbing moor. She saw from there the returning party of shooters and gillies winding its way slowly through the heather, following a burden carried on a stretcher of fir boughs. Some of her women guests were with her, and one of them said afterward that when she first caught sight of the moving figures she got up slowly and crept to the stone balustrade with a crouching movement almost like a young leopardess preparing to spring. But she only watched, making neither sound nor movement until the cortege was near enough for her to see that every man's head was bowed upon his breast, and not one was covered.

Then she said, quite slowly, "They--have--taken off--their bonnets," and fell upon the terrace like a dropped stone.

It was because of this that the girl said that she was dead when I was born. It must have seemed almost as if she were not a living thing. She did not open her eyes or make a sound; she lay white and cold. The celebrated physicians who came from London talked of catalepsy and afterward wrote scientific articles which tried to explain her condition. She did not know when I was born. She died a few minutes after I uttered my first cry.

I know only one thing more, and that Jean Braidfute told me after I grew up. Jean had been my father's nursery governess when he wore his first kilts, and she loved my mother fondly.

"I knelt by her bed and held her hand and watched her face for three hours after they first laid her down," she said. "And my eyes were so near her every moment that I saw a thing the others did not know her well enough, or love her well enough, to see.

"The first hour she was like a dead thing--aye, like a dead thing that had never lived. But when the hand of the clock passed the last second, and the new hour began, I bent closer to her because I saw a change stealing over her. It was not color--it was not even a shadow of a motion. It was something else. If I had spoken what I felt, they would have said I was light-headed with grief and have sent me away. I have never told man or woman. It was my secret and hers. I can tell you, Ysobel. The change I saw was as if she was beginning to listen to something--to listen.

"It was as if to a sound--far, far away at first. But cold and white as stone she lay content, and listened. In the next hour the far-off sound had drawn nearer, and it had become something else--something she saw--something which saw her. First her young marble face had peace in it; then it had joy. She waited in her young stone body until you were born and she could break forth. She waited no longer then.

"Ysobel, my bairn, what I knew was that he had not gone far from the body that had held him when he fell. Perhaps he had felt lost for a bit when he found himself out of it. But soon he had begun to call to her that was like his own heart to him. And she had heard. And then, being half away from earth herself, she had seen him and known he was waiting, and that he would not leave for any far place without her. She was so still that the big doctors thought more than once she had passed. But I knew better."

It was long before I was old enough to be told anything like this that I began to feel that the moor was in secret my companion and friend, that it was not only the moot to me, but something else. It was like a thing alive--a huge giant lying spread out in the sun warming itself, or covering itself with thick, white mist which sometimes writhed and twisted itself into wraiths. First I noticed and liked it some day, perhaps, when it was purple and yellow with gorse and heather and broom, and the honey scents drew bees and butterflies and birds. But soon I saw and was drawn by another thing.

How young was I that afternoon when I sat in the deep window and watched the low, soft whiteness creeping out and hovering over the heather as if the moor had breathed it? I do not remember. It was such a low little mist at first; and it crept and crept until its creeping grew into something heavier and whiter, and it began to hide the heather and the gorse and broom, and then the low young fir-trees. It mounted and mounted, and sometimes a breath of wind twisted it into weird shapes, almost like human creatures. It opened and closed again, and then it dragged and crept and grew thicker. And as I pressed my face against the window-pane, it mounted still higher and got hold of the moor and hid it, hanging heavy and white and waiting. That was what came into my child mind: that it had done what the moor had told it to do; had hidden things which wanted to be hidden, and then it waited.

Strangers say that Muircarrie moor is the most beautiful and the most desolate place in the world, but it never seemed desolate to me. From my first memory of it I had a vague, half-comforted feeling that there was some strange life on it one could not exactly see, but was always conscious of. I know now why I felt this, but I did not know then.

If I had been older when I first began to see what I did see there, I should no doubt have read things in books which would have given rise in my mind to doubts and wonders; but I was only a little child who had lived a life quite apart from the rest of the world. I was too silent by nature to talk and ask questions, even if I had had others to talk to. I had only Jean and Angus, and, as I found out years later, they knew what I did not, and would have put me off with adroit explanations if I had been curious. But I was not curious. I accepted everything as it came and went.

CHAPTER II

I only six when Wee Brown Elspeth was brought to me. Jean and Angus were as fond of each other in their silent way as they were of me, and they often went together with me when I was taken out for my walks. I was kept in the open air a great deal, and Angus would walk by the side of my small, shaggy Shetland pony and lead him over rough or steep places. Sheltie, the pony, was meant for use when we wished to fare farther than a child could walk; but I was trained to sturdy marching and climbing even from my babyhood. Because I so loved the moor, we nearly always rambled there. Often we set out early in the morning, and some simple food was carried, so that we need not return to the castle until we chose. I would ride Sheltie and walk by turns until we found a place I liked; then Jean and Angus would sit down among the heather, Sheltie would be secured, and I would wander about and play in my own way. I do not think it was in a strange way. I think I must have played as almost any lonely little girl might have played. I used to find a corner among the bushes and pretend it was my house and that I had little friends who came to play with me. I only remember one thing which was not like the ordinary playing of children. It was a habit I had of sitting quite still a long time and listening. That was what I called it--"listening." I was listening to hear if the life on the moor made any sound I could understand. I felt as if it might, if I were very still and listened long enough.

Angus and Jean and I were not afraid of rain and mist and change of weather. If we had been we could have had little outdoor life. We always carried plaids enough to keep us warm and dry. So on this day I speak of we did not turn back when we found ourselves in the midst of a sudden mist. We sat down in a sheltered place and waited, knowing it would lift in time. The sun had been shining when we set out.

Angus and Jean were content to sit and guard me while I amused myself. They knew I would keep near them and run into no danger. I was not an adventurous child. I was, in fact, in a more than usually quiet mood that morning. The quiet had come upon me when the mist had begun to creep about and inclose us. I liked it. I liked the sense of being shut in by the soft whiteness I had so often watched from my nursery window in the castle.

"People might be walking about," I said to Angus when he lifted me from Sheltie's back.

"We couldn't see them. They might be walking."

"Nothing that would hurt ye, bairnie," he answered.

"No, they wouldn't hurt me," I said. I had never been afraid that anything on the moor would hurt me.

I played very little that day. The quiet and the mist held me still. Soon I sat down and began to "listen." After a while I knew that Jean and Angus were watching me, but it did not disturb me. They often watched me when they thought I did not know they were doing it.

I had sat listening for nearly half an hour when I heard the first muffled, slow trampling of horses' hoofs. I knew what it was even before it drew near enough for me to be conscious of the other sounds--the jingling of arms and chains and the creaking of leather one notices as troopers pass by. Armed and mounted men were coming toward me. That was what the sounds meant; but they seemed faint and distant, though I knew they were really quite near. Jean and Angus did not appear to hear them. I knew that I only heard them because I had been listening.

Out of the mist they rode a company of wild-looking men wearing garments such as I had never seen before. Most of them were savage and uncouth, and their clothes were disordered and stained as if with hard travel and fight. I did not know--or even ask myself--why they did not frighten me, but they did not. Suddenly I seemed to know that they were brave men and had been doing some brave, hard thing. Here and there among them I caught sight of a broken and stained sword, or a dirk with only a hilt left. They were all pale, but their wild faces were joyous and triumphant. I saw it as they drew near.

The man who seemed their chieftain was a lean giant who was darker but, under his darkness, paler than the rest. On his forehead was a queer, star-shaped scar. He rode a black horse, and before him he held close with his left arm a pretty little girl dressed in strange, rich clothes. The big man's hand was pressed against her breast as he held her; but though it was a large hand, it did not quite cover a dark-red stain on the embroideries of her dress. Her dress was brown, and she had brown hair and soft brown eyes like a little doe's. The moment I saw her I loved her.

The black horse stopped before me. The wild troop drew up and waited behind. The great, lean rider looked at me a moment, and then, lifting the little girl in his long arms, bent down and set her gently on her feet on the mossy earth in the mist beside me. I got up to greet her, and we stood smiling at each other. And in that moment as we stood the black horse moved forward, the muffled trampling began again, the wild company swept on its way, and the white mist closed behind it as if it had never passed.

Of course I know how strange this will seem to people who read it, but that cannot be helped and does not really matter. It was in that way the thing happened, and it did not even seem strange to me. Anything might happen on the moor--anything. And there was the fair little girl with the eyes like a doe's.

I knew she had come to play with me, and we went together to my house among the bushes of broom and gorse and played happily. But before we began I saw her stand and look wonderingly at the dark-red stain on the embroideries on her childish breast. It was as if she were asking herself how it came there and could not understand. Then she picked a fern and a bunch of the thick-growing bluebells and put them in her girdle in such a way that they hid its ugliness.

I did not really know how long she stayed. I only knew that we were happy, and that, though her way of playing was in some ways different from mine, I loved it and her. Presently the mist lifted and the sun shone, and we were deep in a wonderful game of being hidden in a room in a castle because something strange was going to happen which we were not told about. She ran behind a big gorse bush and did not come back. When I ran to look for her she was nowhere. I could not find her, and I went back to Jean and Angus, feeling puzzled.

"Where did she go?" I asked them, turning my head from side to side.

They were looking at me strangely, and both of them were pale. Jean was trembling a little.

"Who was she, Ysobel?" she said.

"The little girl the men brought to play with me," I answered, still looking about me.

"The big one on the black horse put her down--the big one with the star here." I touched my forehead where the queer scar had been.

For a minute Angus forgot himself. Years later he told me.

"Dark Malcolm of the Glen," he broke out. "Wee Brown Elspeth."

"But she is white--quite white!" I said.

"Where did she go?"

Jean swept me in her warm, shaking arms and hugged me close to her breast.

"She's one of the fair ones," she said, kissing and patting me. "She will come again. She'll come often, I dare say. But she's gone now and we must go, too. Get up, Angus, man. We're for the castle."

If we three had been different--if we had ever had the habit of talking and asking questions--we might surely have asked one another questions as I rode on Sheltie's back, with Angus leading us. But they asked me nothing, and I said very little except that I once spoke of the wild-looking horsemen and their pale, joyous faces.

"They were glad," was all I said.

There was also one brief query from Angus.

"Did she talk to you, bairnie?" he said.

I hesitated and stared at him quite a long time. Then I shook my head and answered, slowly, "N-no."

Because I realized then, for the first time, that we had said no words at all. But I had known what she wanted me to understand, and she had known what I might have said to her if I had spoken--and no words were needed. And it was better.

They took me home to the castle, and I was given my supper and put to bed. Jean sat by me until I fell asleep; she was obliged to sit rather a long time, because I was so happy with my memories of Wee Brown Elspeth and the certainty that she would come again. It was not Jean's words which had made me sure. I knew.

She came many times. Through all my childish years I knew that she would come and play with me every few days--though I never saw the wild troopers again or the big, lean man with the scar. Children who play together are not very curious about one another, and I simply accepted her with delight. Somehow I knew that she lived happily in a place not far away. She could come and go, it seemed, without trouble. Sometimes I found her--or she found me upon the moor; and often she appeared in my nursery in the castle. When we were together Jean Braidfute seemed to prefer that we should be alone, and was inclined to keep the under-nurse occupied in other parts of the wing I lived in. I never asked her to do this, but I was glad that it was done. Wee Elspeth was glad, too. After our first meeting she was dressed in soft blue or white, and the red stain was gone; but she was always Wee Brown Elspeth with the doelike eyes and the fair, transparent face, the very fair little face. As I had noticed the strange, clear pallor of the rough troopers, so I noticed that she was curiously fair. And as I occasionally saw other persons with the same sort of fairness, I thought it was a purity of complexion special to some, but not to all. I was not fair like that, and neither was any one else I knew.

CHAPTER III

It was when I was ten years old that Wee Elspeth ceased coming to me, and though I missed her at first, it was not with a sense of grief or final loss. She had only gone somewhere.

It was then that Angus Macayre began to be my tutor. He had been a profound student and had lived among books all his life. He had helped Jean in her training of me, and I had learned more than is usually taught to children in their early years. When a grand governess was sent to Muircarrie by my guardian, she was amazed at the things I was familiar with, but she abhorred the dark, frowning castle and the loneliness of the place and would not stay. In fact, no governess would stay, and so Angus became my tutor and taught me old Gaelic and Latin and Greek, and we read together and studied the ancient books in the library. It was a strange education for a girl, and no doubt made me more than ever unlike others. But my life was the life I loved.

When my guardian decided that I must live with him in London and be educated as modern girls were, I tried to be obedient and went to him; but before two months had passed my wretchedness had made me so ill that the doctor said I should go into a decline and die if I were not sent back to Muircarrie.

"It's not only the London air that seems to poison her," he said when Jean talked to him about me; "it is something else. She will not live, that's all. Sir Ian must send her home."

As I have said before, I had been an unattractive child and I was a plain, uninteresting sort of girl. I was shy and could not talk to people, so of course I bored them. I knew I did not look well when I wore beautiful clothes. I was little and unimportant and like a reed for thinness. Because I was rich and a sort of chieftainess I ought to have been tall and rather stately, or at least I ought to have had a bearing which would have made it impossible for people to quite overlook me. But; any one could overlook me--an insignificant, thin girl who slipped in and out of places and sat and stared and listened to other people instead of saying things herself; I liked to look on and be forgotten. It interested me to watch people if they did not notice me.

Of course, my relatives did not really like me. How could they? They were busy in their big world and did not know what to do with a girl who ought to have been important and was not. I am sure that in secret they were relieved when I was sent back to Muircarrie.

After that the life I loved went on quietly. I studied with Angus, and made the book-walled library my own room. I walked and rode on the moor, and I knew the people who lived in the cottages and farms on the estate. I think they liked me, but I am not sure, because I was too shy to seem very friendly. I was more at home with Feargus, the piper, and with some of the gardeners than I was with any one else. I think I was lonely without knowing; but I was never unhappy. Jean and Angus were my nearest and dearest. Jean was of good blood and a stanch gentlewoman, quite sufficiently educated to be my companion as she had been my early govern-ess.

It was Jean who told Angus that I was giving myself too entirely to the study of ancient books and the history of centuries gone by.

"She is living to-day, and she must not pass through this life without gathering anything from it."

"This life," she put it, as if I had passed through others before, and might pass through others again. That was always her way of speaking, and she seemed quite unconscious of any unusualness in it.

"You are a wise woman, Jean," Angus said, looking long at her grave face. "A wise woman."

He wrote to the London book-shops for the best modern books, and I began to read them. I felt at first as if they plunged me into a world I did not understand, and many of them I could not endure. But I persevered, and studied them as I had studied the old ones, and in time I began to feel as if perhaps they were true. My chief weariness with them came from the way they had of referring to the things I was so intimate with as though they were only the unauthenticated history of a life so long passed by that it could no longer matter to any one. So often the greatest hours of great lives were treated as possible legends. I knew why men had died or were killed or had borne black horror. I knew because I had read old books and manuscripts and had heard the stories which had come down through centuries by word of mouth, passed from father to son.

But there was one man who did not write as if he believed the world had begun and would end with him. He knew he was only one, and part of all the rest. The name I shall give him is Hector MacNairn. He was a Scotchman, but he had lived in many a land. The first time I read a book he had written I caught my breath with joy, again and again. I knew I had found a friend, even though there was no likelihood that I should ever see his face. He was a great and famous writer, and all the world honored him; while I, hidden away in my castle on a rock on the edge of Muircarrie, was so far from being interesting or clever that even in my grandest evening dress and tiara of jewels I was as insignificant as a mouse. In fact, I always felt rather silly when I was obliged to wear my diamonds on state occasions as custom sometimes demanded. Mr. MacNairn wrote essays and poems, and marvelous stories which were always real though they were called fiction. Wheresoever his story was placed--howsoever remote and unknown the scene--it was a real place, and the people who lived in it were real, as if he had some magic power to call up human things to breathe and live and set one's heart beating. I read everything he wrote. I read every word of his again and again. I always kept some book of his near enough to be able to touch it with my hand; and often I sat by the fire in the library holding one open on my lap for an hour or more, only because it meant a warm, close companionship. It seemed at those times as if he sat near me in the dim glow and we understood each other's thoughts without using words, as Wee Brown Elspeth and I had understood--only this was a deeper thing.

I had felt near him in this way for several years, and every year he had grown more famous, when it happened that one June my guardian, Sir Ian, required me to go to London to see my lawyers and sign some important documents connected with the management of the estate. I was to go to his house to spend a week or more, attend a Drawing-Room, and show myself at a few great parties in a proper manner, this being considered my duty toward my relatives. These, I believe, were secretly afraid that if I were never seen their world would condemn my guardian for neglect of his charge, or would decide that I was of unsound mind and intentionally kept hidden away at Muircarrie. He was an honorable man, and his wife was a well-meaning woman. I did not wish to do them an injustice, so I paid them yearly visits and tried to behave as they wished, much as I disliked to be dressed in fine frocks and to wear diamonds on my little head and round my thin neck.

It was an odd thing that this time I found I did not dread the visit to London as much as I usually did. For some unknown reason I became conscious that I was not really reluctant to go. Usually the thought of the days before me made me restless and low-spirited. London always seemed so confused and crowded, and made me feel as if I were being pushed and jostled by a mob always making a tiresome noise. But this time I felt as if I should somehow find a clear place to stand in, where I could look on and listen without being bewildered. It was a curious feeling; I could not help noticing and wondering about it. I knew afterward that it came to me because a change was drawing near. I wish so much that I could tell about it in a better way. But I have only my own way, which I am afraid seems very like a school-girl's. Jean Braidfute made the journey with me, as she always did, and it was like every other journey. Only one incident made it different, and when it occurred there seemed nothing unusual in it. It was only a bit of sad, everyday life which touched me. There is nothing new in seeing a poor woman in deep mourning.

Jean and I had been alone in our railway carriage for a great part of the journey; but an hour or two before we reached London a man got in and took a seat in a corner. The train had stopped at a place where there is a beautiful and well-known cemetery. People bring their friends from long distances to lay them there. When one passes the station, one nearly always sees sad faces and people in mourning on the platform.

There was more than one group there that day, and the man who sat in the corner looked out at them with gentle eyes. He had fine, deep eyes and a handsome mouth. When the poor woman in mourning almost stumbled into the carriage, followed by her child, he put out his hand to help her and gave her his seat. She had stumbled because her eyes were dim with dreadful crying, and she could scarcely see. It made one's heart stand still to see the wild grief of her, and her unconsciousness of the world about her. The world did not matter. There was no world. I think there was nothing left anywhere but the grave she had just staggered blindly away from. I felt as if she had been lying sobbing and writhing and beating the new turf on it with her poor hands, and I somehow knew that it had been a child's grave she had been to visit and had felt she left to utter loneliness when she turned away.

It was because I thought this that I wished she had not seemed so unconscious of and indifferent to the child who was with her and clung to her black dress as if it could not bear to let her go. This one was alive at least, even if she had lost the other one, and its little face was so wistful! It did not seem fair to forget and ignore it, as if it were not there. I felt as if she might have left it behind on the platform if it had not so clung to her skirt that it was almost dragged into the railway carriage with her. When she sank into her seat she did not even lift the poor little thing into the place beside her, but left it to scramble up as best it could. She buried her swollen face in her handkerchief and sobbed in a smothered way as if she neither saw, heard, nor felt any living thing near her.

How I wished she would remember the poor child and let it comfort her! It really was trying to do it in its innocent way. It pressed close to her side, it looked up imploringly, it kissed her arm and her crape veil over and over again, and tried to attract her attention. It was a little, lily-fair creature not more than five or six years old and perhaps too young to express what it wanted to say. It could only cling to her and kiss her black dress, and seem to beg her to remember that it, at least, was a living thing. But she was too absorbed in her anguish to know that it was in the world. She neither looked at nor touched it, and at last it sat with its cheek against her sleeve, softly stroking her arm, and now and then kissing it longingly. I was obliged to turn my face away and look out of the window, because I knew the man with the kind face saw the tears well up into my eyes.

The poor woman did not travel far with us. She left the train after a few stations were passed. Our fellow-traveler got out before her to help her on to the platform. He stood with bared head while he assisted her, but she scarcely saw him. And even then she seemed to forget the child. The poor thing was dragged out by her dress as it had been dragged in. I put out my hand involuntarily as it went through the door, because I was afraid it might fall. But it did not. It turned its fair little face and smiled at me. When the kind traveler returned to his place in the carriage again, and the train left the station, the black-draped woman was walking slowly down the platform and the child was still clinging to her skirt.

CHAPTER IV

My guardian was a man whose custom it was to give large and dignified parties. Among his grand and fashionable guests there was nearly
always a sprinkling of the more important members of the literary
world. The night after I arrived there was to be a particularly notable
dinner. I had come prepared to appear at it. Jean had brought fine array for me and a
case of jewels. I knew I must be "dressed up" and look as important as I could. When
I went up-stairs after tea, Jean was in my room laying things out on the bed.

"The man you like so much is to dine here to-night, Ysobel," she said. "Mr.
Hector MacNairn."

I believe I even put my hand suddenly to my heart as I stood and looked at her,
I was so startled and so glad.

"You must tell him how much you love his books," she said. She had a quiet,
motherly way.

"There will be so many other people who will want to talk to him," I answered,
and I felt a little breathless with excitement as I said it.

"And I should be too shy to know how to say such things properly."

"Don't be afraid of him," was her advice. "The man will be like his books, and
they're the joy of your life."

She made me look as nice as she could in the new dress she had brought; she
made me wear the Muircarrie diamonds and sent me downstairs. It does not matter
who the guests were; I scarcely remember. I was taken in to dinner by a stately elderly man who tried to make me talk, and at last was absorbed by the clever woman
on his other side.

I found myself looking between the flowers for a man's face I could imagine was
Hector MacNairn's. I looked up and down and saw none I could believe belonged

to him. There were handsome faces and individual ones, but at first I saw no Hector MacNairn. Then, on bending forward a little to glance behind an epergne, I found a face which it surprised and pleased me to see. It was the face of the traveler who had helped the woman in mourning out of the railway carriage, baring his head before her grief. I could not help turning and speaking to my stately elderly partner.

"Do you know who that is--the man at the other side of the table?" I asked.

Old Lord Armour looked across and answered with an amiable smile. "It is the author the world is talking of most in these days, and the talking is no new thing. It's Mr. Hector MacNairn."

No one but myself could tell how glad I was. It seemed so right that he should be the man who had understood the deeps of a poor, passing stranger woman's woe. I had so loved that quiet baring of his head! All at once I knew I should not be afraid of him. He would understand that I could not help being shy, that it was only my nature, and that if I said things awkwardly my meanings were better than my words. Perhaps I should be able to tell him something of what his books had been to me. I glanced through the flowers again--and he was looking at me! I could scarcely believe it for a second. But he was. His eyes--his wonderful eyes--met mine. I could not explain why they were wonderful. I think it was the clearness and understanding in them, and a sort of great interestedness. People sometimes look at me from curiosity, but they do not look because they are really interested.

I could scarcely look away, though I knew I must not be guilty of staring. A footman was presenting a dish at my side. I took something from it without knowing what it was. Lord Armour began to talk kindly. He was saying beautiful, admiring things of Mr. MacNairn and his work. I listened gratefully, and said a few words myself now and then. I was only too glad to be told of the great people and the small ones who were moved and uplifted by his thoughts.

"You admire him very much, I can see," the amiable elderly voice said.

I could not help turning and looking up. "It is as if a great, great genius were one's friend--as if he talked and one listened," I said. "He is like a splendid dream which has come true."

Old Lord Armour looked at me quite thoughtfully, as if he saw something new in me.

"That is a good way of putting it, Miss Muircarrie," he answered. "MacNairn would like that. You must tell him about it yourself."

I did not mean to glance through the flowers again, but I did it involuntarily. And I met the other eyes--the wonderful, interested ones just as I had met them before. It almost seemed as if he had been watching me. It might be, I thought, because he only vaguely remembered seeing me before and was trying to recall where we had met.

When my guardian brought his men guests to the drawing-room after dinner, I was looking over some old prints at a quiet, small table. There were a few minutes of smiling talk, and then Sir Ian crossed the room toward me, bringing some one with him. It was Hector MacNairn he brought.

"Mr. MacNairn tells me you traveled together this afternoon without knowing each other," he said. "He has heard something of Muircarrie and would like to hear more, Ysobel. She lives like a little ghost all alone in her feudal castle, Mr. MacNairn. We can't persuade her to like London."

I think he left us alone together because he realized that we should get on better without a companion.

Mr. MacNairn sat down near me and began to talk about Muircarrie. There were very few places like it, and he knew about each one of them. He knew the kind of things Angus Macayre knew--the things most people had either never heard of or had only thought of as legends. He talked as he wrote, and I scarcely knew when he led me into talking also. Afterward I realized that he had asked me questions I could not help answering because his eyes were drawing me on with that quiet, deep interest. It seemed as if he saw something in my face which made him curious.

I think I saw this expression first when we began to speak of our meeting in the railway carriage, and I mentioned the poor little fair child my heart had ached so for.

"It was such a little thing and it did so want to comfort her! Its white little clinging hands were so pathetic when they stroked and patted her," I said. "And she did not even look at it."

He did not start, but he hesitated in a way which almost produced the effect of a start. Long afterward I remembered it.

"The child!" he said. "Yes. But I was sitting on the other side. And I was so absorbed in the poor mother that I am afraid I scarcely saw it. Tell me about it."

"It was not six years old, poor mite," I answered. "It was one of those very fair children one sees now and then. It was not like its mother. She was not one of the White People."

"The White People?" he repeated quite slowly after me. "You don't mean that she was not a Caucasian? Perhaps I don't understand."

That made me feel a trifle shy again. Of course he could not know what I meant. How silly of me to take it for granted that he would!

"I beg pardon. I forgot," I even stammered a little. "It is only my way of thinking of those fair people one sees, those very fair ones, you know--the ones whose fairness looks almost transparent. There are not many of them, of course; but one can't help noticing them when they pass in the street or come into a room. You must have noticed them, too. I always call them, to myself, the White People, because they are different from the rest of us. The poor mother wasn't one, but the child was. Perhaps that was why I looked at it, at first. It was such a lovely little thing; and the whiteness made it look delicate, and I could not help thinking--" I hesitated, because it seemed almost unkind to finish.

"You thought that if she had just lost one child she ought to take more care of the other," he ended for me. There was a deep thoughtfulness in his look, as if he were watching me. I wondered why.

"I wish I had paid more attention to the little creature," he said, very gently. "Did it cry?"

"No," I answered. "It only clung to her and patted her black sleeve and kissed it, as if it wanted to comfort her. I kept expecting it to cry, but it didn't. It made me cry because it seemed so sure that it could comfort her if she would only remember that it was alive and loved her. I wish, I wish death did not make people feel as if it filled all the world--as if, when it happens, there is no life left anywhere. The child who was alive by her side did not seem a living thing to her. It didn't matter."

I had never said as much to any one before, but his watching eyes made me forget my shy worldlessness.

"What do you feel about it--death?" he asked.

The low gentleness of his voice seemed something I had known always.

"I never saw it," I answered. "I have never even seen any one dangerously ill.

I--It is as if I can't believe it."

"You can't believe it? That is a wonderful thing," he said, even more quietly than before.

"If none of us believed, how wonderful that would be! Beautiful, too."

"How that poor mother believed it!" I said, remembering her swollen, distorted, sobbing face. "She believed nothing else; everything else was gone."

"I wonder what would have happened if you had spoken to her about the child?" he said, slowly, as if he were trying to imagine it.

"I'm a very shy person. I should never have courage to speak to a stranger," I answered.

"I'm afraid I'm a coward, too. She might have thought me interfering."

"She might not have understood," he murmured.

"It was clinging to her dress when she walked away down the platform," I went on. "I dare say you noticed it then?"

"Not as you did. I wish I had noticed it more," was his answer. "Poor little White One!"

That led us into our talk about the White People. He said he did not think he was exactly an observant person in some respects. Remembering his books, which seemed to me the work of a man who saw and understood everything in the world, I could not comprehend his thinking that, and I told him so. But he replied that what I had said about my White People made him feel that he must be abstracted sometimes and miss things. He did not remember having noticed the rare fairness I had seen. He smiled as he said it, because, of course, it was only a little thing--that he had not seen that some people were so much fairer than others.

"But it has not been a little thing to you, evidently. That is why I am even rather curious about it," he explained. "It is a difference definite enough to make you speak almost as if they were of a different race from ours."

I sat silent a few seconds, thinking it over. Suddenly I realized what I had never realized before.

"Do you know," I said, as slowly as he himself had spoken, "I did not know that was true until you put it into words. I am so used to thinking of them as different, somehow, that I suppose I do feel as if they were almost like another race, in a way. Perhaps one would feel like that with a native Indian, or a Japanese."

"I dare say that is a good simile," he reflected. "Are they different when you know them well?"

"I have never known one but Wee Brown Elspeth," I answered, thinking it over.

He did start then, in the strangest way.

"What!" he exclaimed. "What did you say?"

I was quite startled myself. Suddenly he looked pale, and his breath caught itself.

"I said Wee Elspeth, Wee Brown Elspeth. She was only a child who played with me," I stammered, "when I was little."

He pulled himself together almost instantly, though the color did not come back to his face at once and his voice was not steady for a few seconds. But he laughed outright at himself.

"I beg your pardon," he apologized. "I have been ill and am rather nervous. I thought you said something you could not possibly have said. I almost frightened you. And you were only speaking of a little playmate. Please go on."

"I was only going to say that she was fair like that, fairer than any one I had ever seen; but when we played together she seemed like any other child. She was the first I ever knew."

I told him about the misty day on the moor, and about the pale troopers and the big, lean leader who carried Elspeth before him on his saddle. I had never talked to any one about it before, not even to Jean Braidfute. But he seemed to be so interested, as if the little story quite fascinated him. It was only an episode, but it brought in the weirdness of the moor and my childish fancies about the things hiding in the white mist, and the castle frowning on its rock, and my baby face pressed against the nursery window in the tower, and Angus and the library, and Jean and her goodness and wise ways. It was dreadful to talk so much about oneself. But he listened so. His eyes never left my face--they watched and held me as if he were enthralled. Sometimes he asked a question.

"I wonder who they were--the horsemen?" he pondered. "Did you ever ask Wee Elspeth?"

"We were both too little to care. We only played," I answered him. "And they came and went so quickly that they were only a sort of dream."

"They seem to have been a strange lot. Wasn't Angus curious about them?" he suggested.

"Angus never was curious about anything," I said. "Perhaps he knew something about them and would not tell me. When I was a little thing I always knew he and Jean had secrets I was too young to hear. They hid sad and ugly things from me, or things that might frighten a child. They were very good."

"Yes, they were good," he said, thoughtfully.

I think any one would have been pleased to find herself talking quietly to a great genius--as quietly as if he were quite an ordinary person; but to me the experience was wonderful. I had thought about him so much and with such adoring reverence. And he looked at me as if he truly liked me, even as if I were something new--a sort of discovery which interested him. I dare say that he had never before seen a girl who had lived so much alone and in such a remote and wild place.

I believe Sir Ian and his wife were pleased, too, to see that I was talking. They were glad that their guests should see that I was intelligent enough to hold the attention even of a clever man. If Hector MacNairn was interested in me I could not be as silly and dull as I looked. But on my part I was only full of wonder and happiness. I was a girl, and he had been my only hero; and it seemed even as if he liked me and cared about my queer life.

He was not a man who had the air of making confidences or talking about himself, but before we parted I seemed to know him and his surroundings as if he had described them. A mere phrase of his would make a picture. Such a few words made his mother quite clear to me. They loved each other in an exquisite, intimate way. She was a beautiful person. Artists had always painted her. He and she were completely happy when they were together. They lived in a house in the country, and I could not at all tell how I discovered that it was an old house with beautiful chimneys and a very big garden with curious high walls with corner towers round it. He only spoke of it briefly, but I saw it as a picture; and always afterward, when I thought of his mother, I thought of her as sitting under a great and ancient apple-tree with the long, late-afternoon shadows stretching on the thick, green grass. I suppose I saw that just because he said:

"Will you come to tea under the big apple-tree some afternoon when the late shadows are like velvet on the grass? That is perhaps the loveliest time."

When we rose to go and join the rest of the party, he stood a moment and glanced round the room at our fellow-guests.

"Are there any of your White People here to-night?" he said, smiling. "I shall begin to look for them everywhere."

I glanced over the faces carelessly. "There are none here to-night," I answered, and then I flushed because he had smiled. "It was only a childish name I gave them," I hesitated. "I forgot you wouldn't understand. I dare say it sounds silly."

He looked at me so quickly.

"No! no! no!" he exclaimed. "You mustn't think that! Certainly not silly."

I do not think he knew that he put out his hand and gently touched my arm, as one might touch a child to make it feel one wanted it to listen.

"You don't know," he said in his low, slow voice, "how glad I am that you have talked to me. Sir Ian said you were not fond of talking to people, and I wanted to know you."

"You care about places like Muircarrie. That is why," I answered, feeling at once how much he understood. "I care for Muircarrie more than for all the rest of the world. And I suppose you saw it in my face. I dare say that the people who love that kind of life cannot help seeing it there."

"Yes," he said, "it is in your eyes. It was what I saw and found myself wondering about when I watched you in the train. It was really the moor and the mist and the things you think are hidden in it."

"Did you watch me?" I asked. "I could not help watching you a little, when you were so kind to the poor woman. I was afraid you would see me and think me rude."

"It was the far look in your face I watched," he said. "If you will come to tea under the big apple-tree I will tell you more about it."

"Indeed I will come," I answered. "Now we must go and sit among the other people--those who don't care about Muircarrie at all."

CHAPTER V

I went to tea under the big apple-tree. It was very big and old and wonderful. No wonder Mr. MacNairn and his mother loved it. Its great branches spread out farther than I had ever seen the branches of an apple-tree spread before. They were gnarled and knotted and beautiful with age. Their shadows upon the grass were velvet, deep and soft. Such a tree could only have lived its life in such a garden. At least it seemed so to me. The high, dim-colored walls, with their curious, low corner towers and the leafage of the wall fruits spread against their brick, inclosed it embracingly, as if they were there to take care of it and its beauty. But the tree itself seemed to have grown there in all its dignified loveliness of shadow to take care of Mrs. MacNairn, who sat under it. I felt as if it loved and was proud of her.

I have heard clever literary people speak of Mrs. MacNairn as a "survival of type." Sometimes clever people bewilder me by the terms they use, but I thought I understood what they meant in her case. She was quite unlike the modern elderly woman, and yet she was not in the least old-fashioned or demodee. She was only exquisitely distinct.

When she rose from her chair under the apple-tree boughs and came forward to meet me that afternoon, the first things which struck me were her height and slenderness and her light step. Then I saw that her clear profile seemed cut out of ivory and that her head was a beautiful shape and was beautifully set. Its every turn and movement was exquisite. The mere fact that both her long, ivory hands enfolded mine thrilled me. I wondered if it were possible that she could be unaware of her loveliness. Beautiful people are thrilling to me, and Mrs. MacNairn has always seemed more so than any one else. This is what her son once said of her:

"She is not merely beautiful; she is Beauty--Beauty's very spirit moving about among us mortals; pure Beauty."

She drew me to a chair under her tree, and we sat down together. I felt as if she were glad that I had come. The watching look I had seen in her son's eyes was in hers also. They watched me as we talked, and I found myself telling her about my home as I had found myself telling him. He had evidently talked to her about it himself. I had never met any one who thought of Muircarrie as I did, but it seemed as if they who were strangers were drawn by its wild, beautiful loneliness as I was.

I was happy. In my secret heart I began to ask myself if it could be true that they made me feel a little as if I somehow belonged to some one. I had always seemed so detached from every one. I had not been miserable about it, and I had not complained to myself; I only accepted the detachment as part of my kind of life.

Mr. MacNairn came into the garden later and several other people came in to tea. It was apparently a sort of daily custom--that people who evidently adored Mrs. MacNairn dropped in to see and talk to her every afternoon. She talked wonderfully, and her friends' joy in her was wonderful, too. It evidently made people happy to be near her. All she said and did was like her light step and the movements of her delicate, fine head--gracious and soft and arrestingly lovely. She did not let me drift away and sit in a corner looking on, as I usually did among strangers. She kept me near her, and in some subtle, gentle way made me a part of all that was happening--the talk, the charming circle under the spreading boughs of the apple-tree, the charm of everything. Sometimes she would put out her exquisite, long-fingered hand and touch me very lightly, and each time she did it I felt as if she had given me new life.

There was an interesting elderly man who came among the rest of the guests. I was interested in him even before she spoke to me of him. He had a handsome, aquiline face which looked very clever. His talk was brilliantly witty. When he spoke people paused as if they could not bear to lose a phrase or even a word. But in the midst of the trills of laughter surrounding him his eyes were unchangingly sad. His face laughed or smiled, but his eyes never.

"He is the greatest artist in England and the most brilliant man," Mrs. MacNairn said to me, quietly. "But he is the saddest, too. He had a lovely daughter who was killed instantly, in his presence, by a fall. They had been inseparable companions and she was the delight of his life. That strange, fixed look has been in his eyes ever since. I know you have noticed it."

We were walking about among the flower-beds after tea, and Mr. MacNairn was showing me a cloud of blue larkspurs in a corner when I saw something which made me turn toward him rather quickly.

"There is one!" I said. "Do look at her! Now you see what I mean! The girl standing with her hand on Mr. Le Breton's arm."

Mr. Le Breton was the brilliant man with the sad eyes. He was standing looking at a mass of white-and-purple iris at the other side of the garden. There were two or three people with him, but it seemed as if for a moment he had forgotten them--had forgotten where he was. I wondered suddenly if his daughter had been fond of irises. He was looking at them with such a tender, lost expression. The girl, who was a lovely, fair thing, was standing quite close to him with her hand in his arm, and she was smiling, too--such a smile!

"Mr. Le Breton!" Mr. MacNairn said in a rather startled tone. "The girl with her hand in his arm?"

"Yes. You see how fair she is," I answered.

"And she has that transparent look. It is so lovely. Don't you think so? SHE is one of the White People."

He stood very still, looking across the flowers at the group. There was a singular interest and intensity in his expression. He watched the pair silently for a whole minute, I think.

"Ye-es," he said, slowly, at last, "I do see what you mean--and it IS lovely. I don't seem to know her well. She must be a new friend of my mother's. So she is one of the White People?"

"She looks like a white iris herself, doesn't she?" I said. "Now you know."

"Yes; now I know," he answered.

I asked Mrs. MacNairn later who the girl was, but she didn't seem to recognize my description of her. Mr. Le Breton had gone away by that time, and so had the girl herself.

"The tall, very fair one in the misty, pale-gray dress," I said. "She was near Mr. Le Breton when he was looking at the iris-bed. You were cutting some roses only a few yards away from her. That VERY fair girl?"

Mrs. MacNairn paused a moment and looked puzzled.

"Mildred Keith is fair," she reflected, "but she was not there then. I don't recall seeing a girl. I was cutting some buds for Mrs. Anstruther. I--" She paused again and turned toward her son, who was standing watching us. I saw their eyes meet in a rather arrested way.

"It was not Mildred Keith," he said. "Miss Muircarrie is inquiring because this girl was one of those she calls the White People. She was not any one I had seen here before."

There was a second's silence before Mrs. MacNairn smilingly gave me one of her light, thrilling touches on my arm.

"Ah! I remember," she said. "Hector told me about the White People. He rather fancied I might be one."

I am afraid I rather stared at her as I slowly shook my head. You see she was almost one, but not quite.

"I was so busy with my roses that I did not notice who was standing near Mr. Le Breton," she said. "Perhaps it was Anabel Mere. She is a more transparent sort of girl than Mildred, and she is more blond. And you don't know her, Hector? I dare say it was she."

CHAPTER VI

I remained in London several weeks. I stayed because the MacNairns were so good to me. I could not have told any one how I loved Mrs. MacNairn, and how different everything seemed when I was with her. I was never shy when we were together. There seemed to be no such thing as shyness in the world. I was not shy with Mr. MacNairn, either. After I had sat under the big apple-tree boughs in the walled garden a few times I realized that I had begun to belong to somebody. Those two marvelous people cared for me in that way--in a way that made me feel as if I were a real girl, not merely a queer little awkward ghost in a far-away castle which nobody wanted to visit because it was so dull and desolate and far from London. They were so clever, and knew all the interesting things in the world, but their cleverness and experience never bewildered or overwhelmed me.

"You were born a wonderful little creature, and Angus Macayre has filled your mind with strange, rich furnishings and marvelous color and form," Mrs. MacNairn actually said to me one day when we were sitting together and she was holding my hand and softly, slowly patting it. She had a way of doing that, and she had also a way of keeping me very near her whenever she could. She said once that she liked to touch me now and then to make sure that I was quite real and would not melt away. I did not know then why she said it, but I understood afterward.

Sometimes we sat under the apple-tree until the long twilight deepened into shadow, which closed round us, and a nightingale that lived in the garden began to sing. We all three loved the nightingale, and felt as though it knew that we were listening to it. It is a wonderful thing to sit quite still listening to a bird singing in the dark, and to dare to feel that while it sings it knows how your soul adores it. It is like a kind of worship.

We had been sitting listening for quite a long time, and the nightingale had just ceased and left the darkness an exquisite silence which fell suddenly but softly as the last note dropped, when Mrs. MacNairn began to talk for the first time of what she called The Fear.

I don't remember just how she began, and for a few minutes I did not quite understand what she meant. But as she went on, and Mr. MacNairn joined in the talk, their meaning became a clear thing to me, and I knew that they were only talking quite simply of something they had often talked of before. They were not as afraid of The Fear as most people are, because they had thought of and reasoned about it so much, and always calmly and with clear and open minds.

By The Fear they meant that mysterious horror most people feel at the thought of passing out of the world they know into the one they don't know at all.

How quiet, how still it was inside the walls of the old garden, as we three sat under the boughs and talked about it! And what sweet night scents of leaves and sleeping flowers were in every breath we drew! And how one's heart moved and lifted when the nightingale broke out again!

"If one had seen or heard one little thing, if one's mortal being could catch one glimpse of light in the dark," Mrs. MacNairn's low voice said out of the shadow near me, "The Fear would be gone forever."

"Perhaps the whole mystery is as simple as this," said her son's voice "as simple as this: that as there are tones of music too fine to be registered by the human ear, so there may be vibrations of light not to be seen by the human eye; form and color as well as sounds; just beyond earthly perception, and yet as real as ourselves, as formed as ourselves, only existing in that other dimension."

There was an intenseness which was almost a note of anguish in Mrs. MacNairn's answer, even though her voice was very low. I involuntarily turned my head to look at her, though of course it was too dark to see her face. I felt somehow as if her hands were wrung together in her lap.

"Oh!" she said, "if one only had some shadow of a proof that the mystery is only that WE cannot see, that WE cannot hear, though they are really quite near us, with us--the ones who seem to have gone away and whom we feel we cannot live without. If once we could be sure! There would be no Fear--there would be none!"

"Dearest"--he often called her "Dearest," and his voice had a wonderful sound in the darkness; it was caress and strength, and it seemed to speak to her of things they knew which I did not--"we have vowed to each other that we WILL believe there is no reason for The Fear. It was a vow between us."

"Yes! Yes!" she cried, breathlessly, "but sometimes, Hector--sometimes--"

"Miss Muircarrie does not feel it--"

"Please say 'Ysobel'!" I broke in. "Please do."

He went on as quietly as if he had not even paused:

"Ysobel told me the first night we met that it seemed as if she could not believe in it."

"It never seems real to me at all," I said. "Perhaps that is because I can never forget what Jean told me about my mother lying still upon her bed, and listening to some one calling her." (I had told them Jean's story a few days before.) "I knew it was my father; Jean knew, too."

"How did you know?" Mrs. MacNairn's voice was almost a whisper.

"I could not tell you that. I never asked myself HOW it was. But I KNEW. We both KNEW. Perhaps"--I hesitated--"it was because in the Highlands people often believe things like that. One hears so many stories all one's life that in the end they don't seem strange. I have always heard them. Those things you know about people who have the second sight. And about the seals who change themselves into men and come on shore and fall in love with girls and marry them. They say they go away now and then, and no one really knows where but it is believed that they go back to their own people and change into seals again, because they must plunge and riot about in the sea. Sometimes they come home, but sometimes they do not.

"A beautiful young stranger, with soft, dark eyes, appeared once not far from Muircarrie, and he married a boatman's daughter. He was very restless one night, and got up and left her, and she never saw him again; but a few days later a splendid dead seal covered with wounds was washed up near his cottage. The fishers say that his people had wanted to keep him from his land wife, and they had fought with him and killed him. His wife had a son with strange, velvet eyes like his father's, and she couldn't keep him away from the water. When he was old enough to swim he swam out one day, because he thought he saw some seals and wanted to get near them. He swam out too far, perhaps. He never came back, and the fishermen said his father's people had taken him. When one has heard stories like that all one's life nothing seems very strange."

"Nothing really IS strange," said Hector MacNairn. "Again and again through all the ages we have been told the secrets of the gods and the wonders of the Law, and we have revered and echoed but never believed. When we believe and know all is simple we shall not be afraid. You are not afraid, Ysobel. Tell my mother you are not."

I turned my face toward her again in the darkness. I felt as if something was going on between them which he somehow knew I could help them in. It was as though he were calling on something in my nature which I did not myself comprehend, but which his profound mind saw and knew was stronger than I was.

Suddenly I felt as if I might trust to him and to It, and that, without being troubled or anxious, I would just say the first thing which came into my mind, because it would be put there for me by some power which could dictate to me. I never felt younger or less clever than I did at that moment; I was only Ysobel Muircarrie, who knew almost nothing. But that did not seem to matter. It was such a simple, almost childish thing I told her. It was only about The Dream.

CHAPTER VII

"The feeling you call The Fear has never come to me," I said to her. "And if it had I think it would have melted away because of a dream I once had. I don't really believe it was a dream, but I call it one. I think I really went somewhere and came back. I often wonder why I came back. It was only a short dream, so simple that there is scarcely anything to tell, and perhaps it will not convey anything to you. But it has been part of my life--that time when I was Out on the Hillside. That is what I call The Dream to myself, 'Out on the Hillside,' as if it were a kind of unearthly poem. But it wasn't. It was more real than anything I have ever felt. It was real--real! I wish that I could tell it so that you would know how real it was."

I felt almost piteous in my longing to make her know. I knew she was afraid of something, and if I could make her know how REAL that one brief dream had been she would not be afraid any more. And I loved her, I loved her so much!

"I was asleep one night at Muircarrie," I went on, "and suddenly, without any preparatory dreaming, I was standing out on a hillside in moonlight softer and more exquisite than I had ever seen or known before. Perhaps I was still in my night-gown--I don't know. My feet were bare on the grass, and I wore something light and white which did not seem to touch me. If it touched me I did not feel it. My bare feet did not feel the grass; they only knew it was beneath them.

"It was a low hill I stood on, and I was only on the side of it. And in spite of the thrilling beauty of the moon, all but the part I stood on melted into soft, beautiful shadow, all below me and above me. But I did not turn to look at or ask myself about anything. You see the difficulty is that there are no earthly words to tell it! All my being was ecstasy--pure, light ecstasy! Oh, what poor words-- But I know no others. If I said that I was happy--HAPPY!--it would be nothing. I WAS happiness itself, I WAS pure rapture! I did not look at the beauty of the night, the sky, the marvelous melting shadow. I was PART of it all, one with it. Nothing held me nothing! The beauty of the night, the light, the air WERE what I was, and I was only thrilling ecstasy and wonder at the rapture of it."

I stopped and covered my face with my hands, and tears wet my fingers.

"Oh, I cannot make it real! I was only there such a short, short time. Even if you had been with me I could not have found words for it, even then. It was such a short time. I only stood and lifted my face and felt the joy of it, the pure marvel of joy. I only heard myself murmuring over and over again: 'Oh, how beautiful! how beautiful! Oh, how BEAUTIFUL!'

"And then a marvel of new joy swept through me. I said, very softly and very slowly, as if my voice were trailing away into silence: 'Oh--h! I--can--lie--down--here--on--the grass--and--sleep . . . all--through--the night--under--this--moon-light. . . . I can sleep--sleep--'

"I began to sink softly down, with the heavenliest feeling of relaxation and repose, as if there existed only the soul of beautiful rest. I sank so softly--and just as my cheek almost touched the grass the dream was over!"

"Oh!" cried Mrs. MacNairn. "Did you awaken?"

"No. I came back. In my sleep I suddenly found myself creeping into my bed again as if I had been away somewhere. I was wondering why I was there, how I had left the hillside, when I had left it. That part WAS a dream--but the other was not. I was allowed to go somewhere--outside--and come back."

I caught at her hand in the dark.

"The words are all wrong," I said. "It is because we have no words to describe that. But have I made you feel it at all? Oh! Mrs. MacNairn, have I been able to make you know that it was not a dream?"

She lifted my hand and pressed it passionately against her cheek, and her cheek, too, was wet--wet.

"No, it was not a dream," she said. "You came back. Thank God you came back, just to tell us that those who do not come back stand awakened in that ecstasy--in that ecstasy. And The Fear is nothing. It is only The Dream. The awakening is out on the hillside, out on the hillside! Listen!" She started as she said it. "Listen! The nightingale is beginning again."

He sent forth in the dark a fountain--a rising, aspiring fountain--of golden notes which seemed to reach heaven itself. The night was made radiant by them. He flung them upward like a shower of stars into the sky. We sat and listened, almost holding our breath. Oh! the nightingale! the nightingale!

"He knows," Hector MacNairn's low voice said, "that it was not a dream."

When there was silence again I heard him leave his chair very quietly.

"Good night! good night!" he said, and went away. I felt somehow that he had left us together for a purpose, but, oh, I did not even remotely dream what the purpose was! But soon she told me, almost in a whisper.

"We love you very much, Ysobel," she said. "You know that?"

"I love you both, with all my heart," I answered. "Indeed I love you."

"We two have been more to each other than mere mother and son. We have been sufficient for each other. But he began to love you that first day when he watched you in the railway carriage. He says it was the far look in your eyes which drew him."

"I began to love him, too," I said. And I was not at all ashamed or shy in saying it.

"We three might have spent our lives together," she went on. "It would have been a perfect thing. But--but--" She stood up as if she could not remain seated. Involuntarily I stood up with her. She was trembling, and she caught and held me in her arms. "He cannot stay, Ysobel," she ended.

I could scarcely hear my own voice when I echoed the words.

"He cannot--stay?"

"Oh! the time will come," she said, "when people who love each other will not be separated, when on this very earth there will be no pain, no grief, no age, no death--when all the world has learned the Law at last. But we have not learned it yet. And here we stand! The greatest specialists have told us. There is some fatal flaw in his heart. At any moment, when he is talking to us, when he is at his work, when he is asleep, he may--cease. It will just be ceasing. At any moment. He cannot stay."

My own heart stood still for a second. Then there rose before me slowly, but clearly, a vision--the vision which was not a dream.

"Out on the hillside," I murmured. "Out on the hillside."

I clung to her with both arms and held her tight. I understood now why they had talked about The Fear. These two who were almost one soul were trying to believe that they were not really to be torn apart--not really. They were trying to heap up for themselves proof that they might still be near each other. And, above all, his effort was to save her from the worst, worst woe. And I understood, too, why something wiser and stronger than myself had led me to tell the dream which was not a dream at all.

But it was as she said; the world had not learned the Secret yet. And there we stood. We did not cry or talk, but we clung to each other--we CLUNG. That is all human creatures can do until the Secret is known. And as we clung the nightingale broke out again.

"O nightingale! O nightingale!" she said in her low wonder of a voice. "WHAT are you trying to tell us!"

CHAPTER VIII

What I feel sure I know by this time is that all the things we think happen by chance and accident are only part of the weaving of the scheme of life. When you begin to suspect this and to watch closely you also begin to see how trifles connect themselves with one another, and seem in the end to have led to a reason and a meaning, though we may not be clever enough to see it clearly. Nothing is an accident. We make everything happen ourselves: the wrong things because we do not know or care whether we are wrong or right, the right ones because we unconsciously or consciously choose the right even in the midst of our ignorance.

I dare say it sounds audacious for an ordinary girl to say such things in an ordinary way; but perhaps I have said them in spite of myself, because it is not a bad thing that they should be said by an every-day sort of person in simple words which other every-day people can understand. I am only expressing what has gradually grown into belief in my mind through reading with Angus ancient books and modern ones--books about faiths and religions, books about philosophies and magics, books about what the world calls marvels, but which are not marvels at all, but only workings of the Law most people have not yet reasoned about or even accepted.

Angus had read and studied them all his life before he began to read them with me, and we talked them over together sitting by the fire in the library, fascinated and staring at each other, I in one high-backed chair and he in another on the opposite side of the hearth. Angus is wonderful--wonderful! He KNOWS there is no such thing as chance. He KNOWS that we ourselves are the working of the Law--and that we ourselves could work what now are stupidly called "miracles" if we could only remember always what the Law is.

What I intended to say at first was merely that it was not by chance that I climbed to the shelf in the library that afternoon and pushed aside the books hiding the old manuscript which told the real story of Dark Malcolm of the Glen and Wee Brown Elspeth. It seemed like chance when it happened, but it was really the first step toward my finding out the strange, beautiful thing I knew soon afterward.

From the beginning of my friendship with the MacNairns I had hoped they would come and stay with me at Muircarrie. When they both seemed to feel such interest in all I told them of it, and not to mind its wild remoteness, I took courage and asked them if they would come to me. Most people are bored by the prospect of life in a feudal castle, howsoever picturesquely it is set in a place where there are no neighbors to count on. Its ancient stateliness is too dull. But the MacNairns were more allured by what Muircarrie offered than they were by other and more brilliant invitations. So when I went back to the castle I was only to be alone a week before they followed me.

Jean and Angus were quite happy in their quiet way when I told them who I was expecting. They knew how glad I was myself. Jean was full of silent pleasure as she arranged the rooms I had chosen for my guests, rooms which had the most sweeping view of the moor. Angus knew that Mr. MacNairn would love the library, and he hovered about consulting his catalogues and looking over his shelves, taking down volumes here and there, holding them tenderly in his long, bony old hand as he dipped into them. He made notes of the manuscripts and books he thought Mr. MacNairn would feel the deepest interest in. He loved his library with all his being, and I knew he looked forward to talking to a man who would care for it in the same way.

He had been going over one of the highest shelves one day and had left his step-ladder leaning against it when he went elsewhere. It was when I mounted the steps, as I often did when he left them, that I came upon the manuscript which related the old story of Dark Malcolm and his child. It had been pushed behind some volumes, and I took it out because it looked so old and yellow. And I opened at once at the page where the tale began.

At first I stood reading, and then I sat down on the broad top of the ladder and forgot everything. It was a savage history of ferocious hate and barbarous reprisals. It had been a feud waged between two clans for three generations. The story of Dark Malcolm and Ian Red Hand was only part of it, but it was a gruesome thing.

Pages told of the bloody deeds they wrought on each other's houses. The one human passion of Dark Malcolm's life was his love for his little daughter. She had brown eyes and brown hair, and those who most loved her called her Wee Brown Elspeth. Ian Red Hand was richer and more powerful than Malcolm of the Glen, and therefore could more easily work his cruel will. He knew well of Malcolm's worship of his child, and laid his plans to torture him through her. Dark Malcolm, coming back to his rude, small castle one night after a raid in which he had lost followers and weapons and strength, found that Wee Brown Elspeth had been carried away, and unspeakable taunts and threats left behind by Ian and his men. With unbound wounds, broken dirks and hacked swords, Dark Malcolm and the remnant of his troop of fighting clansmen rushed forth into the night.

"Neither men nor weapons have we to win her back," screamed Dark Malcolm, raving mad, "but we may die fighting to get near enough to her to drive dirk into her little breast and save her from worse."

They were a band of madmen in their black despair. How they tore through the black night; what unguarded weak spot they found in Ian's castle walls; how they fought their way through it, leaving their dead bodies in the path, none really ever knew. By what strange chance Dark Malcolm came upon Wee Brown Elspeth, craftily set to playing hide-and-seek with a child of Ian's so that she might not cry out and betray her presence; how, already wounded to his death, he caught at and drove his dirk into her child heart, the story only offers guesses at. But kill and save her he did, falling dead with her body held against his breast, her brown hair streaming over it. Not one living man went back to the small, rude castle on the Glen--not one.

I sat and read and read until the room grew dark. When I stopped I found that Angus Macayre was standing in the dimness at the foot of the ladder. He looked up at me and I down at him. For a few moments we were both quite still.

"It is the tale of Ian Red Hand and Dark Malcolm you are reading?" he said, at last.

"And Wee Brown Elspeth, who was fought for and killed," I added, slowly.

Angus nodded his head with a sad face. "It was the only way for a father," he said. "A hound of hell was Ian. Such men were savage beasts in those days, not human."

I touched the manuscript with my hand questioningly. "Did this fall at the back there by accident," I asked, "or did you hide it?"

"I did," he answered. "It was no tale for a young thing to read. I have hidden many from you. You were always poking about in corners, Ysobel."

Then I sat and thought over past memories for a while and the shadows in the room deepened.

"Why," I said, laggingly, after the silence--"why did I call the child who used to play with me 'Wee Brown Elspeth'?"

"It was your own fancy," was his reply. "I used to wonder myself; but I made up my mind that you had heard some of the maids talking and the name had caught your ear. That would be a child's way."

I put my forehead in my hands and thought again. So many years had passed! I had been little more than a baby; the whole thing seemed like a half-forgotten dream when I tried to recall it--but I seemed to dimly remember strange things.

"Who were the wild men who brought her to me first--that day on the moor?" I said. "I do remember they had pale, savage, exultant faces. And torn, stained clothes. And broken dirks and swords. But they were glad of something. Who were they?"

"I did not see them. The mist was too thick," he answered. "They were some wild hunters, perhaps."

"It gives me such a strange feeling to try to remember, Angus," I said, lifting my forehead from my hands.

"Don't try," he said. "Give me the manuscript and get down from the step-ladder. Come and look at the list of books I have made for Mr. MacNairn."

I did as he told me, but I felt as if I were walking in a dream. My mind seemed to have left my body and gone back to the day when I sat a little child on the moor and heard the dull sound of horses' feet and the jingling metal and the creak of leather coming nearer in the thick mist.

I felt as if Angus were in a queer, half-awake mood, too--as if two sets of thoughts were working at the same time in his mind: one his thoughts about Hector MacNairn and the books, the other some queer thoughts which went on in spite of him.

When I was going to leave the library and go up-stairs to dress for dinner he said a strange thing to me, and he said it slowly and in a heavy voice.

"There is a thing Jean and I have often talked of telling you," he said. "We have not known what it was best to do. Times we have been troubled because we could not make up our minds. This Mr. Hector MacNairn is no common man. He is one who is great and wise enough to decide things plain people could not be sure of. Jean and I are glad indeed that he and his mother are coming. Jean can talk to her and I can talk to him, being a man body. They will tell us whether we have been right or wrong and what we must do."

"They are wise enough to tell you anything," I answered. "It sounds as if you and Jean had known some big secret all my life. But I am not frightened. You two would go to your graves hiding it if it would hurt me."

"Eh, bairn!" he said, suddenly, in a queer, moved way. "Eh, bairn!" And he took hold of both my hands and kissed them, pressing them quite long and emotionally to his lips. But he said nothing else, and when he dropped them I went out of the room.

CHAPTER IX

It was wonderful when Mr. MacNairn and his mother came. It was even more beautiful than I had thought it would be. They arrived late in the afternoon, and when I took them out upon the terrace the sun was reddening the moor, and even the rough, gray towers of the castle were stained rose-color. There was that lovely evening sound of birds twittering before they went to sleep in the ivy. The glimpses of gardens below seemed like glimpses of rich tapestries set with jewels. And there was such stillness! When we drew our three chairs in a little group together and looked out on it all, I felt as if we were almost in heaven.

"Yes! yes!" Hector said, looking slowly--round; "it is all here."

"Yes," his mother added, in her lovely, lovely voice. "It is what made you Ysobel."

It was so angelic of them to feel it all in that deep, quiet way, and to think that it was part of me and I a part of it. The climbing moon was trembling with beauty. Tender evening airs quivered in the heather and fern, and the late birds called like spirits.

Ever since the night when Mrs. MacNairn had held me in her arms under the apple-tree while the nightingale sang I had felt toward her son as if he were an archangel walking on the earth. Perhaps my thoughts were exaggerated, but it seemed so marvelous that he should be moving among us, doing his work, seeing and talking to his friends, and yet that he should know that at any moment the great change might come and he might awaken somewhere else, in quite another place. If he had been like other men and I had been like other girls, I suppose that after that night when I heard the truth I should have been plunged into the darkest woe and have almost sobbed myself to death. Why did I not? I do not know except--except that I felt that no darkness could come between us because no darkness could touch him. He could never be anything but alive alive. If I could not see him it would only be because my eyes were not clear and strong enough. I seemed to be waiting for something. I wanted to keep near him.

I was full of this feeling as we sat together on the terrace and watched the moon. I could scarcely look away from him. He was rather pale that evening, but there seemed to be a light behind his pallor, and his eyes seemed to see so much more than the purple and yellow of the heather and gorse as they rested on them.

After I had watched him silently for a little while I leaned forward and pointed to a part of the moor where there was an unbroken blaze of gorse in full bloom like a big patch of gold.

"That is where I was sitting when Wee Brown Elspeth was first brought to me," I said.

He sat upright and looked. "Is it?" he answered. "Will you take me there to-morrow? I have always wanted to see the place."

"Would you like to go early in the morning? The mist is more likely to be there then, as it was that day. It is so mysterious and beautiful. Would you like to do that?" I asked him.

"Better than anything else!" he said. "Yes, let us go in the morning."

"Wee Brown Elspeth seems very near me this evening," I said. "I feel as if--" I broke off and began again. "I have a puzzled feeling about her. This afternoon I found some manuscript pushed behind a book on a high shelf in the library. Angus said he had hidden it there because it was a savage story he did not wish me to read. It was the history of the feud between Ian Red Hand and Dark Malcolm of the Glen. Dark Malcolm's child was called Wee Brown Elspeth hundreds of years ago--five hundred, I think. It makes me feel so bewildered when I remember the one I played with."

"It was a bloody story," he said. "I heard it only a few days before we met at Sir Ian's house in London."

That made me recall something.

"Was that why you started when I told you about Elspeth?" I asked.

"Yes. Perhaps the one you played with was a little descendant who had inherited her name," he answered, a trifle hurriedly. "I confess I was startled for a moment."

I put my hand up to my forehead and rubbed it unconsciously. I could not help seeing a woesome picture.

"Poor little soul, with the blood pouring from her heart and her brown hair spread over her dead father's breast!" I stopped, because a faint memory came back to me. "Mine," I stammered--"mine--how strange!--had a great stain on the embroideries of her dress. She looked at it--and looked. She looked as if she didn't like it--as if she didn't understand how it came there. She covered it with ferns and bluebells."

I felt as if I were being drawn away into a dream. I made a sudden effort to come back. I ceased rubbing my forehead and dropped my hand, sitting upright.

"I must ask Angus and Jean to tell me about her," I said. "Of course, they must have known. I wonder why I never thought of asking questions before."

It was a strange look I met when I involuntarily turned toward him--such an absorbed, strange, tender look!

I knew he sat quite late in the library that night, talking to Angus after his mother and I went to our rooms. Just as I was falling asleep I remember there floated through my mind a vague recollection of what Angus had said to me of asking his advice about something; and I wondered if he would reach the subject in their talk, or if they would spend all their time in poring over manuscripts and books together.

The moor wore its most mysterious look when I got up in the early morning. It had hidden itself in its softest snows of white, swathing mist. Only here and there dark fir-trees showed themselves above it, and now and then the whiteness thinned or broke and drifted. It was as I had wanted him to see it--just as I had wanted to walk through it with him.

We had met in the hall as we had planned, and, wrapped in our plaids because the early morning air was cold, we tramped away together. No one but myself could ever realize what it was like. I had never known that there could be such a feeling of companionship in the world. It would not have been necessary for us to talk at all if we had felt silent. We should have been saying things to each other without words. But we did talk as we walked--in quiet voices which seemed made quieter by the mist, and of quiet things which such voices seemed to belong to.

We crossed the park to a stile in a hedge where a path led at once on to the moor. Part of the park itself had once been moorland, and was dark with slender firs and thick grown with heather and broom. On the moor the mist grew thicker, and if I had not so well known the path we might have lost ourselves in it. Also I knew by heart certain little streams that rushed and made guiding sounds which were sometimes loud whispers and sometimes singing babbles. The damp, sweet scent of fern and heather was in our nostrils; as we climbed we breathed its freshness.

"There is a sort of unearthly loveliness in it all," Hector MacNairn said to me. His voice was rather like his mother's. It always seemed to say so much more than his words.

"We might be ghosts," I answered. "We might be some of those the mist hides because they like to be hidden."

"You would not be afraid if you met one of them?" he said.

"No. I think I am sure of that. I should feel that it was only like myself, and, if I could hear, might tell me things I want to know."

"What do you want to know?" he asked me, very low. "You!"

"Only what everybody wants to know--that it is really AWAKENING free, ready for wonderful new things, finding oneself in the midst of wonders. I don't mean angels with harps and crowns, but beauty such as we see now; only seeing it without burdens of fears before and behind us. And knowing there is no reason to be afraid. We have all been so afraid. We don't know how afraid we have been--of everything."

I stopped among the heather and threw my arms out wide. I drew in a great, joyous morning breath.

"Free like that! It is the freeness, the light, splendid freeness, I think of most."

"The freeness!" he repeated. "Yes, the freeness!"

"As for beauty," I almost whispered, in a sort of reverence for visions I remembered, "I have stood on this moor a thousand times and seen loveliness which made me tremble. One's soul could want no more in any life. But 'Out on the Hillside' I KNEW I was part of it, and it was ecstasy. That was the freeness."

"Yes--it was the freeness," he answered.

We brushed through the heather and the bracken, and flower-bells shook showers of radiant drops upon us. The mist wavered and sometimes lifted before us, and opened up mystic vistas to veil them again a few minutes later. The sun tried to break through, and sometimes we walked in a golden haze.

We fell into silence. Now and then I glanced sidewise at my companion as we made our soundless way over the thick moss. He looked so strong and beautiful. His tall body was so fine, his shoulders so broad and splendid! How could it be! How could it be! As he tramped beside me he was thinking deeply, and he knew he need not talk to me. That made me glad--that he should know me so well and feel me so near. That was what he felt when he was with his mother, that she understood and that at times neither of them needed words.

Until we had reached the patch of gorse where we intended to end our walk we did not speak at all. He was thinking of things which led him far. I knew that, though I did not know what they were. When we reached the golden blaze we had seen the evening before it was a flame of gold again, because--it was only for a few moments--the mist had blown apart and the sun was shining on it.

As we stood in the midst of it together--Oh! how strange and beautiful it was!--Mr. MacNairn came back. That was what it seemed to me--that he came back. He stood quite still a moment and looked about him, and then he stretched out his arms as I had stretched out mine. But he did it slowly, and a light came into his face.

"If, after it was over, a man awakened as you said and found himself--the self he knew, but light, free, splendid--remembering all the ages of dark, unknowing dread, of horror of some black, aimless plunge, and suddenly seeing all the childish uselessness of it--how he would stand and smile! How he would stand and SMILE!"

Never had I understood anything more clearly than I understood then. Yes, yes! That would be it. Remembering all the waste of fear, how he would stand and SMILE!

He was smiling himself, the golden gorse about him already losing its flame in the light returning mist-wraiths closing again over it, when I heard a sound far away and high up the moor. It sounded like the playing of a piper. He did not seem to notice it.

"We shall be shut in again," he said. "How mysterious it is, this opening and closing! I like it more than anything else. Let us sit down, Ysobel."

He spread the plaid we had brought to sit on, and laid on it the little strapped basket Jean had made ready for us. He shook the mist drops from our own plaids, and as I was about to sit down I stopped a moment to listen.

"That is a tune I never heard on the pipes before," I said. "What is a piper doing out on the moor so early?"

He listened also. "It must be far away. I don't hear it," he said. "Perhaps it is a bird whistling."

"It is far away," I answered, "but it is not a bird. It's the pipes, and playing such a strange tune. There! It has stopped!"

But it was not silent long; I heard the tune begin again much nearer, and the piper was plainly coming toward us. I turned my head.

The mist was clearing, and floated about like a thin veil through which one could see objects. At a short distance above us on the moor I saw something moving. It was a man who was playing the pipes. It was the piper, and almost at once I knew him, because it was actually my own Feargus, stepping proudly through the heather with his step like a stag on the hills. His head was held high, and his face had a sort of elated delight in it as if he were enjoying himself and the morning and the music in a new way. I was so surprised that I rose to my feet and called to him.

"Feargus!" I cried. "What--"

I knew he heard me, because he turned and looked at me with the most extraordinary smile. He was usually a rather grave-faced man, but this smile had a kind of startling triumph in it. He certainly heard me, for he whipped off his bonnet in a salute which was as triumphant as the smile. But he did not answer, and actually passed in and out of sight in the mist.

When I rose Mr. MacNairn had risen, too. When I turned to speak in my surprise, he had fixed on me his watchful look.

"Imagine its being Feargus at this hour!" I exclaimed. "And why did he pass by in such a hurry without answering? He must have been to a wedding and have been up all night. He looked--" I stopped a second and laughed.

"How did he look?" Mr. MacNairn asked.

"Pale! That won't do--though he certainly didn't look ill." I laughed again. "I'm laughing because he looked almost like one of the White People."

"Are you sure it was Feargus?" he said.

"Quite sure. No one else is the least like Feargus. Didn't you see him yourself?"

"I don't know him as well as you do; and there was the mist," was his answer. "But he certainly was not one of the White People when I saw him last night."

I wondered why he looked as he did when he took my hand and drew me down to my place on the plaid again. He did not let it go when he sat down by my side. He held it in his own large, handsome one, looking down on it a moment or so; and then he bent his head and kissed it long and slowly two or three times.

"Dear little Ysobel!" he said. "Beloved, strange little Ysobel."

"Am I strange!" I said, softly.

"Yes, thank God!" he answered.

I had known that some day when we were at Muircarrie together he would tell me what his mother had told me--about what we three might have been to one another. I trembled with happiness at the thought of hearing him say it himself. I knew he was going to say it now.

He held my hand and stroked it. "My mother told you, Ysobel--what I am waiting for?" he said.

"Yes."

"Do you know I love you?" he said, very low.

"Yes. I love you, too. My whole life would have been heaven if we could always have been together," was my answer.

He drew me up into his arms so that my cheek lay against his breast as I went on, holding fast to the rough tweed of his jacket and whispering: "I should have belonged to you two, heart and body and soul. I should never have been lonely again. I should have known nothing, whatsoever happened, but tender joy."

"Whatsoever happened?" he murmured.

"Whatsoever happens now, Ysobel, know nothing but tender joy. I think you CAN. 'Out on the Hillside!' Let us remember."

"Yes, yes," I said; "'Out on the Hillside.'" And our two faces, damp with the sweet mist, were pressed together.

CHAPTER X

The mist had floated away, and the moor was drenched with golden sunshine when we went back to the castle. As we entered the hall I heard the sound of a dog howling, and spoke of it to one of the men-servants who had opened the door.

"That sounds like Gelert. Is he shut up somewhere?"

Gelert was a beautiful sheep-dog who belonged to Feargus and was his heart's friend. I allowed him to be kept in the courtyard.

The man hesitated before he answered me, with a curiously grave face.

"It is Gelert, miss. He is howling for his master. We were obliged to shut him in the stables."

"But Feargus ought to have reached here by this time," I was beginning.

I was stopped because I found Angus Macayre almost at my elbow. He had that moment come out of the library. He put his hand on my arm.

"Will ye come with me?" he said, and led me back to the room he had just left. He kept his hand on my arm when we all stood together inside, Hector and I looking at him in wondering question. He was going to tell me something--we both saw that.

"It is a sad thing you have to hear," he said. "He was a fine man, Feargus, and a most faithful servant. He went to see his mother last night and came back late across the moor. There was a heavy mist, and he must have lost his way. A shepherd found his body in a tarn at daybreak. They took him back to his father's home."

I looked at Hector MacNairn and again at Angus. "But it couldn't be Feargus," I cried. "I saw him an hour ago. He passed us playing on his pipes. He was playing a new tune I had never heard before a wonderful, joyous thing. I both heard and SAW him!"

Angus stood still and watched me. They both stood still and watched me, and even in my excitement I saw that each of them looked a little pale.

"You said you did not hear him at first, but you surely saw him when he passed so near," I protested. "I called to him, and he took off his bonnet, though he did not stop. He was going so quickly that perhaps he did not hear me call his name."

What strange thing in Hector's look checked me? Who knows?

"You DID see him, didn't you?" I asked of him.

Then he and Angus exchanged glances, as if asking each other to decide some grave thing. It was Hector MacNairn who decided it.

"No," he answered, very quietly, "I neither saw nor heard him, even when he passed. But you did."

"I did, quite plainly," I went on, more and more bewildered by the way in which they kept a sort of tender, awed gaze fixed on me. "You remember I even noticed that he looked pale. I laughed, you know, when I said he looked almost like one of the White People--"

Just then my breath caught itself and I stopped. I began to remember things--hundreds of things.

Angus spoke to me again as quietly as Hector had spoken.

"Neither Jean nor I ever saw Wee Brown Elspeth," he said--"neither Jean nor I. But you did. You have always seen what the rest of us did not see, my bairn--always."

I stammered out a few words, half in a whisper. "I have always seen what you others could not see? WHAT--HAVE--I--SEEN?"

But I was not frightened. I suppose I could never tell any one what strange, wide, bright places seemed suddenly to open and shine before me. Not places to shrink back from--oh no! no! One could be sure, then--SURE! Feargus had lifted his bonnet with that extraordinary triumph in his look--even Feargus, who had been rather dour.

"You called them the White People," Hector MacNairn said.

Angus and Jean had known all my life. A very old shepherd who had looked in my face when I was a baby had said I had the eyes which "SAW." It was only the saying of an old Highlander, and might not have been remembered. Later the two began to believe I had a sight they had not. The night before Wee Brown Elspeth had been brought to me Angus had read for the first time the story of Dark Malcolm, and as they sat near me on the moor they had been talking about it. That was why he forgot himself when I came to ask them where the child had gone, and told him of the big, dark man with the scar on his forehead. After that they were sure.

They had always hidden their knowledge from me because they were afraid it might frighten me to be told. I had not been a strong child. They kept the secret from my relatives because they knew they would dislike to hear it and would not believe, and also would dislike me as a queer, abnormal creature. Angus had fears of what they might do with doctors and severe efforts to obliterate from my mind my "nonsense," as they would have been sure to call it. The two wise souls had shielded me on every side.

"It was better that you should go on thinking it only a simple, natural thing," Angus said. "And as to natural, what IS natural and what is not? Man has not learned all the laws of nature yet. Nature's a grand, rich, endless thing, always unrolling her scroll with writings that seem new on it. They're not new. They were always written there. But they were not unrolled. Never a law broken, never a new law, only laws read with stronger eyes."

Angus and I had always been very fond of the Bible--the strange old temple of wonders, full of all the poems and tragedies and histories of man, his hates and battles and loves and follies, and of the Wisdom of the universe and the promises of the splendors of it, and which even those of us who think ourselves the most believing neither wholly believe nor will understand. We had pored over and talked of it. We had never thought of it as only a pious thing to do. The book was to us one of the mystic, awe-inspiring, prophetic marvels of the world.

That was what made me say, half whispering: "I have wondered and wondered what it meant--that verse in Isaiah: 'Behold the former things are come to pass and new things do I declare; before they spring forth I tell you of them.' Perhaps it means only the unrolling of the scroll."

"Aye, aye!" said Angus; "it is full of such deep sayings, and none of us will listen to them."

"It has taken man eons of time," Hector MacNairn said, thinking it out as he spoke--"eons of time to reach the point where he is beginning to know that in every stock and stone in his path may lie hidden some power he has not yet dreamed of. He has learned that lightning may be commanded, distance conquered, motion chained and utilized; but he, the one CONSCIOUS force, has never yet begun to suspect that of all others he may be the one as yet the least explored. How do we know that there does not lie in each of us a wholly natural but, so far, dormant power of sight--a power to see what has been called The Unseen through all the Ages whose sightlessness has made them Dark? Who knows when the Shadow around us may begin to clear? Oh, we are a dull lot--we human things--with a queer, obstinate conceit of ourselves."

"Complete we think we are," Angus murmured half to himself. "Finished creatures! And look at us! How many of us in a million have beauty and health and full power? And believing that the law is that we must crumple and go to pieces hour by hour! Who'd waste the time making a clock that went wrong as often? Nay, nay! We shall learn better than this as time goes on. And we'd better be beginning and setting our minds to work on it. 'Tis for us to do--the minds of us. And what's the mind of us but the Mind that made us? Simple and straight enough it is when once you begin to think it out. The spirit of you sees clearer than we do, that's all," he said to me. "When your mother brought you into the world she was listening to one outside calling to her, and it opened the way for you."

At night Hector MacNairn and his mother and I sat on the terrace under stars which seemed listening things, and we three drew nearer to one another, and nearer and nearer.

"When the poor mother stumbled into the train that day," was one of the things Hector told me, "I was thinking of The Fear and of my own mother. You looked so slight and small as you sat in your corner that I thought at first you were almost a child. Then a far look in your eyes made me begin to watch you. You were so sorry for the poor woman that you could not look away from her, and something in your face touched and puzzled me. You leaned forward suddenly and put out your hand protectingly as she stepped down on to the platform.

"That night when you spoke quite naturally of the child, never doubting that I had seen it, I suddenly began to suspect. Because of The Fear"--he hesitated--"I had been reading and thinking many things new to me. I did not know what I believed. But you spoke so simply, and I knew you were speaking the truth. Then you spoke just as naturally of Wee Brown Elspeth. That startled me because not long before I had been told the tale in the Highlands by a fine old story-teller who is the head of his clan. I saw you had never heard the story before. And yet you were telling me that you had played with the child."

"He came home and told me about you," Mrs. MacNairn said. "His fear of The Fear was more for me than for himself. He knew that if he brought you to me, you who are more complete than we are, clearer-eyed and nearer, nearer, I should begin to feel that he was not going--out. I should begin to feel a reality and nearness myself. Ah, Ysobel! How we have clung to you and loved you! And then that wonderful afternoon! I saw no girl with her hand through Mr. Le Breton's arm; Hector saw none. But you saw her. She was THERE!"

"Yes, she was there," I answered. "She was there, smiling up at him. I wish he could have known."

What does it matter if this seems a strange story? To some it will mean something; to some it will mean nothing. To those it has a meaning for it will open wide windows into the light and lift heavy loads. That would be quite enough, even if the rest thought it only the weird fancy of a queer girl who had lived alone and given rein to her silliest imaginings. I wanted to tell it, howsoever poorly and ineffectively it was done. Since I KNEW I have dropped the load of ages--the black burden. Out on the hillside my feet did not even feel the grass, and yet I was standing, not floating. I had no wings or crown. I was only Ysobel out on the hillside, free!

This is the way it all ended.

For three weeks that were like heaven we three lived together at Muircarrie. We saw every beauty and shared every joy of sun and dew and love and tender understanding.

After one lovely day we had spent on the moor in a quiet dream of joy almost strange in its perfectness, we came back to the castle; and, because the sunset was of such unearthly radiance and changing wonder we sat on the terrace until the last soft touch of gold had died out and left the pure, still, clear, long summer twilight.

When Mrs. MacNairn and I went in to dress for dinner, Hector lingered a little behind us because the silent beauty held him.

I came down before his mother did, and I went out upon the terrace again because I saw he was still sitting there. I went to the stone balustrade very quietly and leaned against it as I turned to look at him and speak.

Then I stood quite still and looked long--for some reason not startled, not anguished, not even feeling that he had gone. He was more beautiful than any human creature I had ever seen before. But It had happened as they said it would. He had not ceased--but something else had. Something had ceased.

It was the next evening before I came out on the terrace again. The day had been more exquisite and the sunset more wonderful than before. Mrs. MacNairn was sitting by her son's side in the bedroom whose windows looked over the moor. I am not going to say one word of what had come between the two sunsets. Mrs. MacNairn and I had clung--and clung. We had promised never to part from each other. I did not quite know why I went out on the terrace; perhaps it was because I had always loved to sit or stand there.

This evening I stood and leaned upon the balustrade, looking out far, far, far over the moor. I stood and gazed and gazed. I was thinking about the Secret and the Hillside. I was very quiet--as quiet as the twilight's self. And there came back to me the memory of what Hector had said as we stood on the golden patch of gorse when the mist had for a moment or so blown aside, what he had said of man's awakening, and, remembering all the ages of--childish, useless dread, how he would stand-- I did not turn suddenly, but slowly. I was not startled in the faintest degree. He stood there close to me as he had so often stood.

And he stood--and smiled.

I have seen him many times since. I shall see him many times again. And when I see him he always stands--and smiles.

The Codes Of Hammurabi And Moses
W. W. Davies

QTY

The discovery of the Hammurabi Code is one of the greatest achievements of archaeology, and is of paramount interest, not only to the student of the Bible, but also to all those interested in ancient history...

Religion   **ISBN:** *1-59462-338-4*   **Pages:132**

MSRP $12.95

The Theory of Moral Sentiments
Adam Smith

QTY

This work from 1749. contains original theories of conscience amd moral judgment and it is the foundation for systemof morals.

Philosophy **ISBN:** *1-59462-777-0*   **Pages:536**

MSRP $19.95

Jessica's First Prayer
Hesba Stretton

QTY

In a screened and secluded corner of one of the many railway-bridges which span the streets of London there could be seen a few years ago, from five o'clock every morning until half past eight, a tidily set-out coffee-stall, consisting of a trestle and board, upon which stood two large tin cans, with a small fire of charcoal burning under each so as to keep the coffee boiling during the early hours of the morning when the work-people were thronging into the city on their way to their daily toil...

Pages:84

Childrens   **ISBN:** *1-59462-373-2*   *MSRP $9.95*

My Life and Work
Henry Ford

QTY

Henry Ford revolutionized the world with his implementation of mass production for the Model T automobile. Gain valuable business insight into his life and work with his own auto-biography... "We have only started on our development of our country we have not as yet, with all our talk of wonderful progress, done more than scratch the surface. The progress has been wonderful enough but..."

Pages:300

Biographies/ **ISBN:** *1-59462-198-5*   *MSRP $21.95*

The Art of Cross-Examination
Francis Wellman

QTY

I presume it is the experience of every author, after his first book is published upon an important subject, to be almost overwhelmed with a wealth of ideas and illustrations which could readily have been included in his book, and which to his own mind, at least, seem to make a second edition inevitable. Such certainly was the case with me; and when the first edition had reached its sixth impression in five months, I rejoiced to learn that it seemed to my publishers that the book had met with a sufficiently favorable reception to justify a second and considerably enlarged edition. ..

Reference   **ISBN: *1-59462-647-2***

Pages:412

MSRP $19.95

On the Duty of Civil Disobedience
Henry David Thoreau

QTY

Thoreau wrote his famous essay, On the Duty of Civil Disobedience, as a protest against an unjust but popular war and the immoral but popular institution of slave-owning. He did more than write—he declined to pay his taxes, and was hauled off to gaol in consequence. Who can say how much this refusal of his hastened the end of the war and of slavery ?

Law   **ISBN: *1-59462-747-9***

Pages:48

MSRP $7.45

Dream Psychology Psychoanalysis for Beginners
Sigmund Freud

QTY

Sigmund Freud, born Sigismund Schlomo Freud (May 6, 1856 - September 23, 1939), was a Jewish-Austrian neurologist and psychiatrist who co-founded the psychoanalytic school of psychology. Freud is best known for his theories of the unconscious mind, especially involving the mechanism of repression; his redefinition of sexual desire as mobile and directed towards a wide variety of objects; and his therapeutic techniques, especially his understanding of transference in the therapeutic relationship and the presumed value of dreams as sources of insight into unconscious desires.

Psychology   **ISBN: *1-59462-905-6***

Pages:196

MSRP $15.45

The Miracle of Right Thought
Orison Swett Marden

QTY

Believe with all of your heart that you will do what you were made to do. When the mind has once formed the habit of holding cheerful, happy, prosperous pictures, it will not be easy to form the opposite habit. It does not matter how improbable or how far away this realization may see, or how dark the prospects may be, if we visualize them as best we can, as vividly as possible, hold tenaciously to them and vigorously struggle to attain them, they will gradually become actualized, realized in the life. But a desire, a longing without endeavor, a yearning abandoned or held indifferently will vanish without realization.

Pages:360

Self Help   **ISBN: *1-59462-644-8***

MSRP $25.45

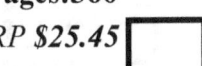

www.bookjungle.com *email: sales@bookjungle.com fax: 630-214-0564 mail: Book Jungle PO Box 2226 Champaign, IL 61825*

QTY

The Rosicrucian Cosmo-Conception Mystic Christianity by *Max Heindel*   ISBN: *1-59462-188-8*   **$38.95**
The Rosicrucian Cosmo-conception is not dogmatic, neither does it appeal to any other authority than the reason of the student. It is: not controversial, but is: sent forth in the, hope that it may help to clear...   New Age/Religion Pages 646

Abandonment To Divine Providence by *Jean-Pierre de Caussade*   ISBN: *1-59462-228-0*   **$25.95**
"The Rev. Jean Pierre de Caussade was one of the most remarkable spiritual writers of the Society of Jesus in France in the 18th Century. His death took place at Toulouse in 1751. His works have gone through many editions and have been republished...   Inspirational/Religion Pages 400

Mental Chemistry by *Charles Haanel*   ISBN: *1-59462-192-3*   **$23.95**
Mental Chemistry allows the change of material conditions by combining and appropriately utilizing the power of the mind. Much like applied chemistry creates something new and unique out of careful combinations of chemicals the mastery of mental chemistry...   New Age Pages 354

The Letters of Robert Browning and Elizabeth Barret Barrett 1845-1846 vol II   ISBN: *1-59462-193-4*   **$35.95**
by *Robert Browning* and *Elizabeth Barrett*   Biographies Pages 596

Gleanings In Genesis (volume I) by *Arthur W. Pink*   ISBN: *1-59462-130-6*   **$27.45**
Appropriately has Genesis been termed "the seed plot of the Bible" for in it we have, in germ form, almost all of the great doctrines which are afterwards fully developed in the books of Scripture which follow...   Religion/Inspirational Pages 420

The Master Key by *L. W. de Laurence*   ISBN: *1-59462-001-6*   **$30.95**
In no branch of human knowledge has there been a more lively increase of the spirit of research during the past few years than in the study of Psychology, Concentration and Mental Discipline. The requests for authentic lessons in Thought Control, Mental Discipline and...   New Age/Business Pages 422

The Lesser Key Of Solomon Goetia by *L. W. de Laurence*   ISBN: *1-59462-092-X*   **$9.95**
This translation of the first book of the "Lernegton" which is now for the first time made accessible to students of Talismanic Magic was done, after careful collation and edition, from numerous Ancient Manuscripts in Hebrew, Latin, and French...   New Age/Occult Pages 92

Rubaiyat Of Omar Khayyam by *Edward Fitzgerald*   ISBN:*1-59462-332-5*   **$13.95**
Edward Fitzgerald, whom the world has already learned, in spite of his own efforts to remain within the shadow of anonymity, to look upon as one of the rarest poets of the century, was born at Bredfield, in Suffolk, on the 31st of March, 1809. He was the third son of John Purcell...   Music Pages 172

Ancient Law by *Henry Maine*   ISBN: *1-59462-128-4*   **$29.95**
The chief object of the following pages is to indicate some of the earliest ideas of mankind, as they are reflected in Ancient Law, and to point out the relation of those ideas to modern thought.   Religion/History Pages 452

Far-Away Stories by *William J. Locke*   ISBN: *1-59462-129-2*   **$19.45**
"Good wine needs no bush, but a collection of mixed vintages does. And this book is just such a collection. Some of the stories I do not want to remain buried for ever in the museum files of dead magazine-numbers an author's not unpardonable vanity..."   Fiction Pages 272

Life of David Crockett by *David Crockett*   ISBN: *1-59462-250-7*   **$27.45**
"Colonel David Crockett was one of the most remarkable men of the times in which he lived. Born in humble life, but gifted with a strong will, an indomitable courage, and unremitting perseverance...   Biographies/New Age Pages 424

Lip-Reading by *Edward Nitchie*   ISBN: *1-59462-206-X*   **$25.95**
Edward B. Nitchie, founder of the New York School for the Hard of Hearing, now the Nitchie School of Lip-Reading, Inc, wrote "LIP-READING Principles and Practice". The development and perfecting of this meritorious work on lip-reading was an undertaking...   How-to Pages 400

A Handbook of Suggestive Therapeutics, Applied Hypnotism, Psychic Science   ISBN: *1-59462-214-0*   **$24.95**
by *Henry Munro*   Health/New Age/Health/Self-help Pages 376

A Doll's House: and Two Other Plays by *Henrik Ibsen*   ISBN: *1-59462-112-8*   **$19.95**
Henrik Ibsen created this classic when in revolutionary 1848 Rome. Introducing some striking concepts in playwriting for the realist genre, this play has been studied the world over.   Fiction/Classics/Plays 308

The Light of Asia by *sir Edwin Arnold*   ISBN: *1-59462-204-3*   **$13.95**
In this poetic masterpiece, Edwin Arnold describes the life and teachings of Buddha. The man who was to become known as Buddha to the world was born as Prince Gautama of India but he rejected the worldly riches and abandoned the reigns of power when...   Religion/History/Biographies Pages 170

The Complete Works of Guy de Maupassant by *Guy de Maupassant*   ISBN: *1-59462-157-8*   **$16.95**
"For days and days, nights and nights, I had dreamed of that first kiss which was to consecrate our engagement, and I knew not on what spot I should put my lips..."   Fiction/Classics Pages 240

The Art of Cross-Examination by *Francis L. Wellman*   ISBN: *1-59462-309-0*   **$26.95**
Written by a renowned trial lawyer, Wellman imparts his experience and uses case studies to explain how to use psychology to extract desired information through questioning.   How-to/Science/Reference Pages 408

Answered or Unanswered? by *Louisa Vaughan*   ISBN: *1-59462-248-5*   **$10.95**
Miracles of Faith in China   Religion Pages 112

The Edinburgh Lectures on Mental Science (1909) by *Thomas*   ISBN: *1-59462-008-3*   **$11.95**
This book contains the substance of a course of lectures recently given by the writer in the Queen Street Hail, Edinburgh. Its purpose is to indicate the Natural Principles governing the relation between Mental Action and Material Conditions...   New Age/Psychology Pages 148

Ayesha by *H. Rider Haggard*   ISBN: *1-59462-301-5*   **$24.95**
Verily and indeed it is the unexpected that happens! Probably if there was one person upon the earth from whom the Editor of this, and of a certain previous history, did not expect to hear again...   Classics Pages 380

Ayala's Angel by *Anthony Trollope*   ISBN: *1-59462-352-X*   **$29.95**
The two girls were both pretty, but Lucy who was twenty-one who supposed to be simple and comparatively unattractive, whereas Ayala was credited, as her Bombwhat romantic name might show, with poetic charm and a taste for romance. Ayala when her father died was nineteen...   Fiction Pages 484

The American Commonwealth by *James Bryce*   ISBN: *1-59462-286-8*   **$34.45**
An interpretation of American democratic political theory. It examines political mechanics and society from the perspective of Scotsman James Bryce   Politics Pages 572

Stories of the Pilgrims by *Margaret P. Pumphrey*   ISBN: *1-59462-116-0*   **$17.95**
This book explores pilgrims religious oppression in England as well as their escape to Holland and eventual crossing to America on the Mayflower, and their early days in New England...   History Pages 268

QTY

The Fasting Cure *by Sinclair Upton*　　　　　　　　　ISBN: *1-59462-222-1*　**$13.95**
*In the Cosmopolitan Magazine for May, 1910, and in the Contemporary Review (London) for April, 1910, I published an article dealing with my experi-
ences in fasting. I have written a great many magazine articles, but never one which attracted so much attention... New Age/Self Help/Health Pages 164*

Hebrew Astrology *by Sepharial*　　　　　　　　　　ISBN: *1-59462-308-2*　**$13.45**
*In these days of advanced thinking it is a matter of common observation that we have left many of the old landmarks behind and that we are now pressing
forward to greater heights and to a wider horizon than that which represented the mind-content of our progenitors... Astrology Pages 144*

Thought Vibration or The Law of Attraction in the Thought World　　ISBN: *1-59462-127-6*　**$12.95**
by William Walker Atkinson　　　　　　　　　　　　　　　*Psychology/Religion Pages 144*

Optimism *by Helen Keller*　　　　　　　　　　　　ISBN: *1-59462-108-X*　**$15.95**
*Helen Keller was blind, deaf, and mute since 19 months old, yet famously learned how to overcome these handicaps, communicate with the world, and
spread her lectures promoting optimism. An inspiring read for everyone... Biographies/Inspirational Pages 84*

Sara Crewe *by Frances Burnett*　　　　　　　　　　ISBN: *1-59462-360-0*　**$9.45**
*In the first place, Miss Minchin lived in London. Her home was a large, dull, tall one, in a large, dull square, where all the houses were alike, and all the
sparrows were alike, and where all the door-knockers made the same heavy sound... Childrens/Classic Pages 88*

The Autobiography of Benjamin Franklin *by Benjamin Franklin*　　ISBN: *1-59462-135-7*　**$24.95**
*The Autobiography of Benjamin Franklin has probably been more extensively read than any other American historical work, and no other book of its kind
has had such ups and downs of fortune. Franklin lived for many years in England, where he was agent...　Biographies/History Pages 332*

Name	
Email	
Telephone	
Address	
City, State ZIP	

☐ **Credit Card**　　　　　☐ **Check / Money Order**

Credit Card Number	
Expiration Date	
Signature	

Please Mail to:　Book Jungle
PO Box 2226
Champaign, IL 61825
or Fax to:　　　630-214-0564

ORDERING INFORMATION

web*: www.bookjungle.com*
email*: sales@bookjungle.com*
fax*: 630-214-0564*
mail*: Book Jungle PO Box 2226 Champaign, IL 61825*
or PayPal *to sales@bookjungle.com*

Please contact us for bulk discounts

DIRECT-ORDER TERMS

**20% Discount if You Order
Two or More Books**
Free Domestic Shipping!
Accepted: Master Card, Visa,
Discover, American Express